Mama's and Great-Grammaw's gentle fingers weave the design and their lulling voices weave the tale as they braid their children's hair into the striking cornrow patterns of Africa.

Every design has a name and means something in the powerful past and present richness of the Black tradition. As Mama and Great-Grammaw work, Sister and little brother MeToo learn what wealth is theirs to share, just for the braiding.

"Camille Yarbrough is a poet, griot and storyteller who has crafted a special, rhythmic and moving story for you and yours.... The illustrations by Carole Byard dignify and give all due respect to the story!"

—*Council on Interracial Books for Children*

CORNROWS

by Camille Yarbrough · illustrated by Carole Byard

The Putnam & Grosset Group

A PaperStar Book, published in 1996 by The Putnam & Grosset Group,
345 Hudson Street, New York, NY 10014. PaperStar is a
registered trademark of The Putnam Berkley Group, Inc.
The PaperStar logo is a trademark of The Putnam Berkley Group, Inc.
Originally published in 1979 by Coward, McCann & Geoghegan, Inc.
Published simultaneously in Canada.
Manufactured in China
Library of Congress Cataloging-in-Publication Data
Yarbrough, Camille. Summary: Explains how the hairstyle of corncrows,
a symbol of Africa since ancient times, can today in this country
symbolize the courage of outstanding Afro-Americans.
[1. Afro-Americans—Fiction.   2. Hair—Fiction.]
I. Byard, Carole M.   II. Title.   PZ7.Y1955Co   [E] 78-24010
ISBN 0-698-11436-1
9   10   8

To Mama and Daddy
who did what they could
in their day
in their way
to pass on to their children
the spirit of
what could be
would be
tomorrow

Hi, my name is Sister. My other name is Shirley Ann, but everybody calls me Sister. This is my little brother, Mike. Everybody calls him Brother just like they call me Sister. Mama says that's the way they do, down south, where she was born. But you know what? I call Brother MeToo. That's because everything I do, he has to do too.

Like when Mama says I can go out to play till it gets dark? MeToo has to say, "Can I go, too?" He's such a baby. But we have good times.

Now we're goin inside to hear one of Mama and Great-Grammaw's stories. Every evening we have storytellin time. And uuuu-uuuu-uuuh! Mama and Great-Grammaw, they tell some se-ri-ous, dy-no-mite stories.

Like yesterday when we went in, Great-Grammaw was fixin Mama's hair in cornrows. That's what Great-Grammaw calls those braids. She said the braids got that name because our old folks down south planted rows of corn in the fields. And the rows in the cornfields looked like the rows of braids that they fixed in their hair. Mama's hair was lookin pretty.

So I said, "Fix my hair in braids, Great-Grammaw."

And MeToo said, "Fix my hair in braids, Great-Grammaw."

Then I said, "What's the name of your style, Ma?"

And ol' MeToo said, "Please, Ma, what's the name of yours?"

Well, Mama and Great-Grammaw started laughin. They were feelin good, because every day when Mama comes home from work, they get together and have a lot of fun talkin about what's goin on at church and rememberin and laughin about when they lived down in Alabama.

Sometimes we don't even have to ask to go out and play. Because Great-Grammaw says, "You kids go on out an play, now."

Anyhow, Mama's hair was ready, and she stood up and turned around in front of the mirror like she was goin to dance or somethin. Showin off in her new pretty dress that Daddy bought her. Then she bent down and kissed me on the head. And she said:

> I delight in tellin you, my child—
> yes, you please me when you ask it—
> it's a hairstyle that's called *suku*.
> in Yoruba, it means *basket*.

MeToo said, "Basket?"

Great-Grammaw said, "Yes, basket."

Then ol silly MeToo looked at me and said, "You gonna be a basket head." Then he fell out on the floor laughin. But Great-Grammaw said, "Brother!" And he got up quick, because he knew Great-Grammaw would get on his case.

I asked Mama, "What will you put in the basket, Mama?"

And she said, "I think I'll put love."

Then ol knock-kneed MeToo asked Great-Grammaw, "What will you put in my basket, Great-Grammaw?"

And Great-Grammaw said, "I think I'll put love."

Then he asked her, "If I fall down, will the love go away, Great-Grammaw?"

"Oh, nooo, my darlin!" she said. "Because the love, like the basket, will be a part of you."

So I asked, "What kind of love will you put in the basket, Great-Grammaw?"

And she said, "Hand-me-down love, baby."

And of course MeToo had to ask, "What kind of love will you put in my basket, Great-Grammaw?"

"Hand-me-down love, dumplin," she said.

Then Great-Grammaw picked MeToo up and hugged him in her lap and started hummin just like she does when we're in church. She said, "An if you fall down, that ol hand-me-down love won't go nowhere. Because it's gonna be a part of you. Just like the basket I'm fixin to braid in ya hair."

Then Mama told me to bring the stool and come sit down so she could fix my hair. Mama and Great-Grammaw always sing a little bit before they tell their stories. They say that's so they can get in the mood.

When I heard Mama start singin real quick, I sat down on the stool in front of her and said, "Mama, tell me a story about cornrowed hair."

And real quick, MeToo looked up at Great-Grammaw and said, "Great-Grammaw, tell me a story about cornrowed hair, too." And Mama started singin:

> Uuuum, I'm tellin a story about cornrowed
> hair. . . .

An Great-Grammaw said:

> Um, um, um, um, um.
> I'm tellin a story about cornrowed hair. . . .

Then Great-Grammaw put MeToo down on his little chair so she could get at his head, and she said:

> Child, come an sit by my knee,
> an I will tell you about your family tree.
> An I will dress you
> as a prince should be,
> an the right name will come
> to both you an me.
> An I will braid your hair,
> an I will braid your hair. . . .

We were real quiet then. And Great-Grammaw started tellin the story:

"There is a spirit that lives inside of you. It keeps on growin. It never dies. Sometimes, when you're afraid, it trembles. An sometimes, when you're hurt an ready to give up, it barely flickers. But it keeps growin. It never dies. Now a long, long time ago, in a land called Africa, our ancient people worked through that spirit. To give life meanin. An to give praise. An through their spirit gave form to symbols of courage, an honor, an wisdom, an love, an strength. Symbols which live forever. Just to give praise."

Then Mama said:

Some symbols took form in royal stools,

and others took form in sculptured ware,

and some took form in ritual masquerade,

and some took form in braided hair.

MeToo asked Mama, "Who was wearin the braided hair?"

"Ooh, lots of people," Mama said. "Everywhere you looked. Almost everyone that you would see. People from Egypt to Swaziland. From Senegal to Somali."

You could tell the clan, the village,
by the style of hair they wore. . . .
Then the Yoruba people
were wearin thirty braids and more. . . .
You would know the princess, queen, and
   bride
by number of the braid. . . .
You would know the gods they worshiped
by the pattern that they made.

"Then a terrible thing happened."
I said, "What, Mama?"

The clan,
the village,
the priest,
the bride,
the royalty,
all were packed into the slaver ships
and brought across the sea . . .
where they trembled on the auction block
and on the chain-gang line . . .
where they flickered on the pyre
and while hangin from the pine. . . .
And the style that once was praise
then was changed to one of shame.
Then the meanings were forgotten
and forgotten was the name. . . .

MeToo asked Great-Grammaw, "Did the spirit die?"
And Great-Grammaw said:

> No such thing!
> If you're quiet
> you can still hear the royal rhythms,
> still feel the spirit in the air.
> Look around an you will see the old, old
>   symbol
> that we now call cornrowed hair. . . .
> You see, the spirit of the symbol
> is not changed by time, place, class, or fame,
> an not even by hate or shame,
> oh noo. . . . You see,
> it's the spirit that makes the symbol
> an the spirit goes by many names.

Then Mama said:

> Little girl, little boy,
> let's play the hair name game . . .
> every day a different style,
> every day a different name. . . .

MeToo said, "Me first! Me first! Where can I get a name, Great-Grammaw?"

Great-Grammaw said, "She's gonna tell you. Listen to ya mother."

And Mama said:

> You can name it for a river,
> you can name it for a flower,
> for the year, for the month,
> for the day or for the hour.

We started clappin, and Great-Grammaw said, "Keep ya head still, boy."

> You can name it for a poem,
> for a city, for a school.
> You can name it for your teacher
> or for the golden rule.
> You can name it for a hero,
> for a proverb or a fish.
> You can name it for a star,
> for a song or for a wish. . . .

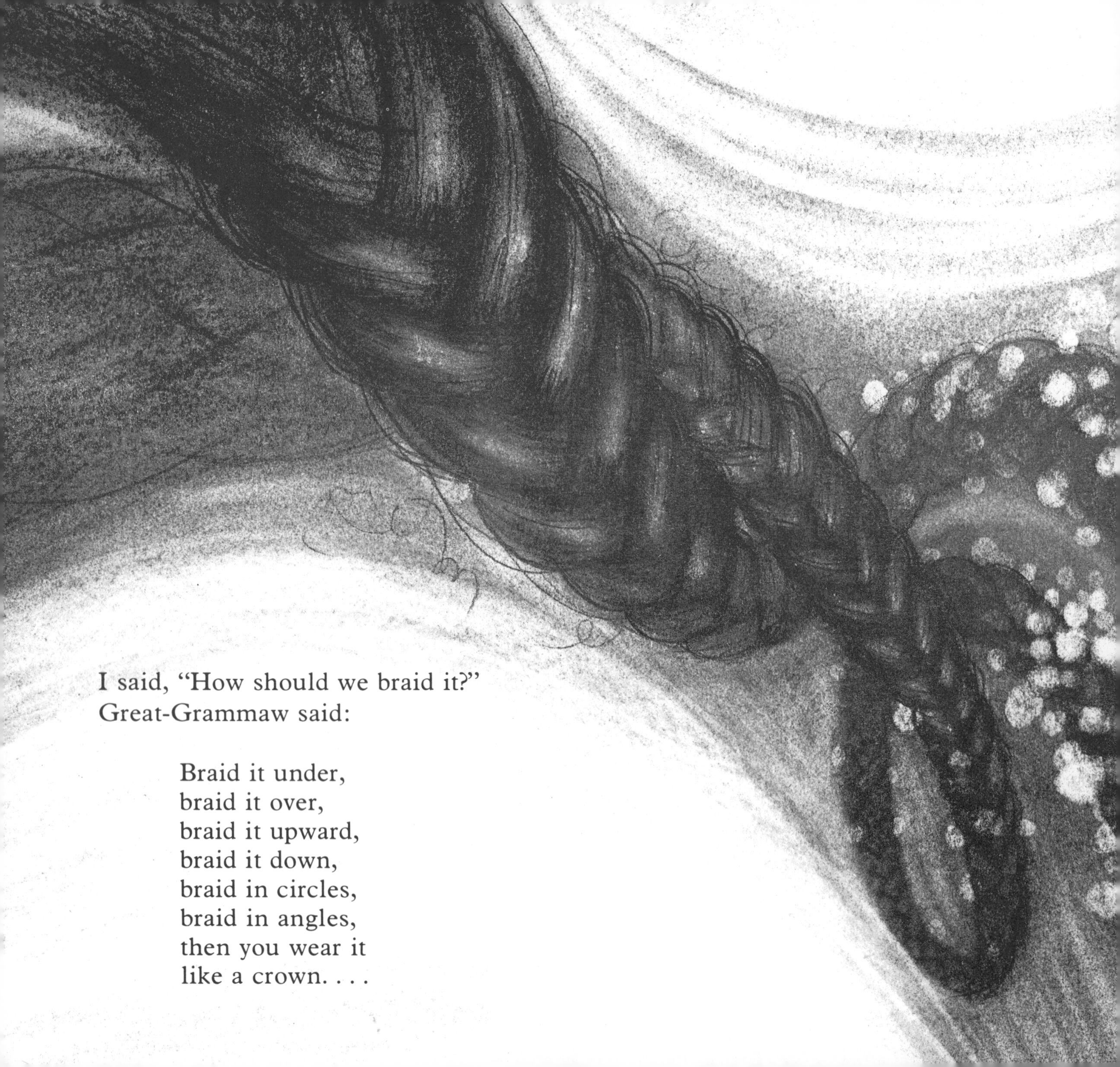

I said, "How should we braid it?"
Great-Grammaw said:

Braid it under,
braid it over,
braid it upward,
braid it down,
braid in circles,
braid in angles,
then you wear it
like a crown. . . .

I said, "How should we style it?"
Great-Grammaw said:

Style it fancy,
style it simple,
style with seeds an cowry shells.
Style with ribbons,
style with ivory,
style with beads an tinkly bells. . . .

MeToo said, "What should we name it, Mama?"
Mama said:

> Name it Robeson,
> name it Malcolm,
> you can name it Dr. King.
> Name it DuBois,
> name it Garvey,
> name it something you can sing.
>
> Name it Tubman,
> name it Hamer,
> oh, you can style a Fannie Lou.
> Name it Nzinga,
> Rosa Parks,
> and please name it Hatshepsut, too. . . .

Name it Powell,
name it Carver,
Richard Wright and Langston Hughes.
Name it Belafonte,
name it Baldwin,
name it glory,
name it blues. . . .

Name it Miriam
Katherine Dunham,
Mary Bethune and Josephine.
Name it Aretha,
name it Nina,
name it priestess,
name it queen. . . .

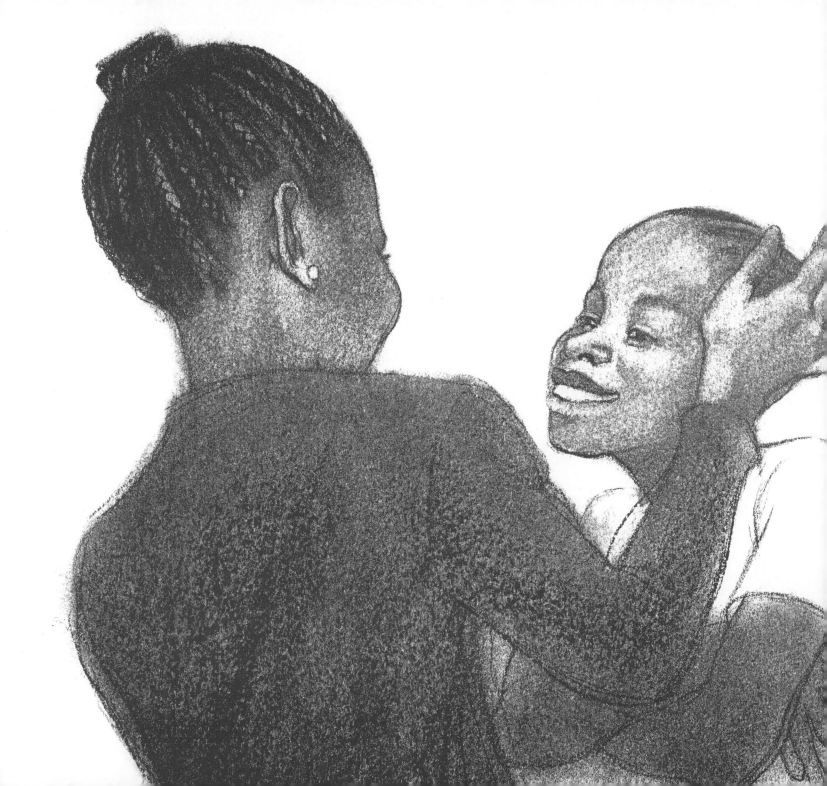

By that time I had some serious cornrows. So did MeToo.

Great-Grammaw said:

> Little girl, little boy,
> with the cornrowed style,
> let me see your pretty face,
> let me see your handsome smile.
> Now . . . what are you goin to name it?

I named mine after Langston Hughes, because I can say one of his poems. MeToo named his after Batman. He's such a baby.

Then Daddy came home from work and he said we looked so fine that after we ate our dinner, he was goin to take us all out to hear some sounds. And he did, too.

About the Author

In addition to writing, Camille Yarbrough has had a distinguished career as an actress, composer, and singer. She has appeared often on television and in theater, in a wide variety of roles, and was a member of both the New York and touring companies of *To Be Young, Gifted, and Black*. She has made a recording of her songs and dialogues, *The Iron Pot Cooker*, which has received excellent reviews, and she was recently awarded a Jazz/Folk/Ethnic Performance Fellowship Grant by the National Endowment for the Arts.

A native of Chicago, Ms. Yarbrough now makes her home in New York City.

About the Illustrator

Carole Byard was born in Atlantic City, New Jersey, and she studied at the Fleischer Art Memorial in Philadelphia and at the New York Phoenix School of Design. Ms. Byard is well known for her paintings, and she has illustrated many books for children, including *Africa Dream* by Eloise Greenfield and, most recently, *Three African Tales* by Adjai Robinson. Her paintings have appeared in many exhibitions, both solo and group, and she is active in art education programs in the New York area.